Chickens Lay Eggs- Not Rabbits!!

by Nancy Stearns Theiss, Ph.D.
Lauren Theiss, Illustrator

First published by Dog Ear Publishing
4011 Vincennes Rd
Indianapolis, IN 46268
www.dogearpublishing.net

ISBN: 978-1-4575-3349-4

This book is printed on acid-free paper.

Printed in the United States of America

Peck was born on WinnRose Farm
and was very proud to be a chicken!

Even though she was just a little fluffy chick she had great pride knowing one day she would grow up, lay eggs and help feed her farm family that took care of her and the other flock of chickens.

It took a long time for Peck to get her real feathers- they were quite beautiful! Shiny, red, brown and black.

One of the farm people, a small girl named Lida, would pet Peck every day. Peck loved to be petted and would run up to Lida everytime Lida came around the chicken yard.

Peck often sat in Lida's lap while Lida fed her special table scraps like **spaghetti** noodles- the noodles looked like worms that Peck would scratch and eat from the ground, but they tasted even better.

Peck also loved sweets and sometimes Lida
would give her special treats like bits of

cake and
cookies

Finally, after Peck waited and waited, she grew up into a beautiful hen and she began laying eggs!

Peck laid beautiful, **brown** eggs with deep yellow yolks!

Each day when Peck laid an egg, Lida would come and gather it up—Lida would pet Peck and give her a special treat!

As Spring rolled around, Peck turned one year old. One day Lida picked Peck up and talked about the Easter bunny coming to her house and leaving a basket of Easter Eggs! Peck was confused- rabbits don't lay eggs!!!!! How could rabbits be in charge of Easter Eggs!

Peck began to worry as Easter approached.
What could Peck do? Lida needs to know-
Chickens Lay Eggs- Not Rabbits!!

Peck decided she would make her own Easter
Basket for Lida. Each day Peck would walk around
the farm and gather beautiful mosses and
wildflowers. Then she wove them in and out of
twigs until there was a beautiful basket that
looked just like Springtime!

Two days before Easter Peck found a whole field full of **purple** violets- she ate , and ate, and ate- as many **purple** violets as she could hold!!

The next day Peck laid the most beautiful, big **purple** egg that had ever been laid at WinnRose farm! She carefully rolled it into the Easter Basket and waited for Lida to come to the hen house.

On Easter morning Lida ran to the hen house to feed the chickens- when she opened the door-

WHAT A SURPRISE!!

The most beautiful purple egg in the most beautiful Easter basket that Lida had ever seen!!!

"Oh Peck!!" Lida yelled!, " I told everyone I knew that chickens laid eggs, not rabbits!!! Peck just clucked and winked!!

CPSIA information can be obtained
at www.ICGtesting.com
Printed in the USA
BVOW11s1416190118
505336BV00005B/20/P

9 781457 543494